Ting's Subway Mystery

By Selina Li Bi, M.F.A.
Illustrated by Luke Scriven

Publishing Credits

Rachelle Cracchiolo, M.S.Ed., *Publisher*
Aubrie Nielsen, M.S.Ed., *EVP of Content Development*
Emily R. Smith, M.A.Ed., *VP of Content Development*
Véronique Bos, *Creative Director*
Dani Neiley, *Associate Editor*
Kevin Pham, *Graphic Designer*

Image Credits

Illustrated by Luke Scriven

Library of Congress Cataloging-in-Publication Data

Names: Bjorlie, Selina Libi, author. | Scriven, Luke, illustrator.
Title. Ting's subway mystery / by Selina Li Bi, M.F.A. ; Illustrated by Luke Scriven.
Description: Huntington Beach, CA : Teacher Created Materials, [2022] | Audience: Grades 2-3. | Summary: ""On the way to school, Ting becomes intrigued with a woman who always sits across from her on the subway. One day, the woman is not there, but she leaves something behind. Ting sets out to find the woman and return it""-- Provided by publisher.
Identifiers: LCCN 2021052853 (print) | LCCN 2021052854 (ebook) | ISBN 9781087601908 (paperback) | ISBN 9781087631950 (ebook)
Subjects: LCSH: Readers (Primary) | LCGFT: Readers (Publications)
Classification: LCC PE1119.2 .B568 2022 (print) | LCC PE1119.2 (ebook) | DDC 428.6/2--dc23/eng/20211104
LC record available at https://lccn.loc.gov/2021052853
LC ebook record available at https://lccn.loc.gov/2021052854"

5482 Argosy Avenue
Huntington Beach, CA 92649
www.tcmpub.com

ISBN 978-1-0876-0190-8

Table of Contents

Chapter One

Window Flowers

Every afternoon, Ting rode the subway with her mom. She dreaded the ride home from school. It took forever, and it was boring.

They sat in the same seats, across from a woman who reminded Ting of her *amah*, her grandmother. The woman had gray hair just like Amah and small brown eyes. But the woman never smiled. Amah always smiled, no matter what.

Ting tried not to stare at the woman, but she couldn't help it. The woman wore a scarf around her neck. It was torn and ragged. She smelled funny too—like the herbs Amah boiled when someone was sick. Today, the woman was really busy.

Snip, snip. Her scissors made a cutting sound as they sliced into a red paper square. Colorful pieces of paper fell in a pile on her lap. When the woman was done, she held up the paper. Light shone through the holes. It was a flower!

She's just like Amah, Ting thought. *She makes wonderful things appear with her hands.*

When Amah visited, she made delicious dumplings appear. Ting made them disappear by eating them!

The following day, Ting decided to finally talk to the woman on the subway.

"What are you making?" Ting asked. She stared at the bright square in the woman's hands.

The woman didn't look up. She seemed really crabby. "Wait and see," she said with an impatient voice.

Ting wished she hadn't talked to the woman.

The woman kept cutting. *Snip, snip.* A few minutes later, she unfolded the paper. It was a beautiful butterfly.

"That's amazing," said Ting. "Why are you making these?"

"I decorate windows," said the woman. "These are called *window flowers*. It is an old tradition. It started thousands of years ago in China."

The woman got off the train before Ting and her mom. Ting waved goodbye.

Chapter Two

Gone

The next afternoon, Ting waited on the subway platform with her mom. When the train stopped, she noticed a bright object on one of its windows. It was the paper butterfly!

Ting rushed onto the subway car. She couldn't wait to see the woman. They sat in their usual seats, but to Ting's surprise, the seat across from them was empty!

Where could she be? What if something happened to her? Ting's mind spun. *And she left her window flower!*

She pulled the butterfly off the window, folded it, and placed it gently into her backpack. She decided to give it to the woman the next day.

But the following day, the woman was still not on the subway. Her seat was empty. Ting's heart started to pound.

She tugged at her mom's sleeve and whispered, "Where is she?"

"Where is who?" asked Mom.

"The woman who always sits over there and makes window flowers. Do you think something happened to her?" asked Ting.

Mom shrugged and squeezed Ting's hand. "I don't know. You worry too much."

Ting felt silly. She didn't even know the woman's name. All she knew was that the woman reminded her of Amah, even if she was sort of crabby. Ting decided to become a detective and find her!

She tried to remember when the woman got off the subway. It was usually right before her. Yes, in fact, it was the next stop.

"We need to find the missing woman," said Ting as she turned to her mom. She pulled out the paper butterfly from her backpack. "She left this, and I have to give it back to her."

The subway came to a stop. Ting grabbed Mom's hand and pulled. "This is her stop!"

"What are you doing?" asked Mom, dashing after Ting.

"We're going to find that woman," said Ting. "There's no time to waste!"

Chapter Three

Clues

Ting and her mom got off the train. They walked down the street, past the shops that lined the sidewalks. They stopped at a pet store. Dogs barked and fish swam in tanks with waving seaweed.

Ting searched the aisles with no luck.

"We're never going to find her," Ting finally said.

"We should go back," said Mom.

"No, I'm not giving up," replied Ting as she peered out the window.

A lovely red paper flower clung to the glass. It was just like the one the woman made on the subway. Her first clue! She was close.

They continued down the sidewalk, and Ting kept thinking about the paper butterfly. She had to find the woman.

Something caught Ting's attention—a ragged pink scarf lying on the sidewalk outside a used bookstore. She picked it up, and it smelled exactly like the woman on the subway.

"A second clue!" she said to Mom, waving the torn scarf in the air.

"Are you sure that's hers?" asked Mom.

"I'm positive," said Ting as she dashed into the bookstore.

Inside, the air was musty, and books were piled high on tables. Yet there was no sign of the missing woman.

Ting went to the front counter. "Do you know who owns this scarf? She makes window flowers."

The man behind the counter glanced up. "Yes, she comes here to buy paper." He winked and said, "You'll find her one block from here. Can't miss it."

"Good work, detective," said Mom.

After all this walking, Ting started to get tired.

"Third clue!" Mom said with excitement, stopping in front of a store with a dusty window.

It was covered with paper designs of flowers and animals, just like the ones the woman made.

Inside, the air had an earthy odor. Jars filled with various dried herbs lined the shelves. It was a Chinese grocery store.

Someone approached, but it was not the person Ting expected.

Chapter Four

Surprises

"Can I help you?" asked a teenage girl.

"I'm looking for the woman who makes those window decorations. Here's her scarf," said Ting.

The girl took the scarf and said, "You mean Lily? I'll go get her." She disappeared into the back of the store.

What if it isn't the missing woman? thought Ting.

A few moments later, the woman from the subway appeared with the scarf around her neck.

The mystery was solved, and the woman's name was Lily!

"I'm so glad Ting the detective found you," said Mom.

"Thank you for my scarf, but why are you here?" asked Lily.

Ting reached into her backpack and pulled out the paper butterfly. "I found this too. Is it yours?" she said.

Without a smile, Lily said, "No, it is not."

"But I saw you making it on the subway," said Ting.

"Yes, but I left it on the window for you," said Lily.

"For me?" replied Ting.

"You seemed so interested, and you remind me of my grandchild," said Lily. "I just went to see her." For the first time, the woman smiled. She had a few missing teeth.

Maybe that's why she doesn't usually smile, thought Ting.

"You remind me of my amah," said Ting. "She lives far away, across the ocean. She left a week ago, and I really miss her."

"Tape the butterfly to your window, and light will shine through it. It will remind you of your amah," said Lily.

"It's beautiful," said Ting.

"Come sit, and I'll show you how to cut window flowers," replied Lily.

"That sounds great," said Ting as she turned to her mom. "I'm glad we looked for Lily."

"Me too," said Lily.

About Us

The Author
Selina Li Bi likes to dream and write. She has two dogs as writing pals. Her characters are sometimes braver than she is.

The Illustrator
One of Luke Scriven's goals as an illustrator is to make viewers say "awww," which they do regularly. He studied animation and has developed a style that is well suited for children's illustrations. His grandmother encouraged him to draw and paint as a child. She told him, "You have to use the white of the paper to your advantage."